Nothing Strikes Back

Keith Hale

Nothing Strikes Back

Chapter One

The young man who opened the door for me had to be the best-looking human on the planet. I was at his house to pick up a girl, most likely his sister. I had asked her out on a whim, and she had smiled and said yes, also on a whim it seemed to me, but in any case, here I was.

"Hi. Hailey here?" I asked.

The boy was looking at me in the same way that I suspected I was looking at him, kind of dazzled by an unexpected pleasure. That didn't figure. I was good-looking myself, maybe, but not *that* good looking. Not like him. Just average good looks like Hailey.

"Yeah," he said. "She said she was going out with a new guy tonight. I guess that's you."

"I guess it is."

"You sure you're not used?"

Handsome kid and clever too.

"I have been."

The boy smiled. Lovely smile. "Sorry to hear that. Come in. I'll get her."

New guy, huh? Whatever. New guy, new girl. I had finally gotten over the last girl who dumped me, one in a long string. I was getting pretty fed up with girls, actually, but there was something about Hailey I liked. She was worth a try.

While the boy went upstairs, a woman came in from another part of the house and introduced herself as Hailey's mother. She seemed pleased with my appearance, but I was used to that. I basically look like a nice guy, and I like to think I am. Nothing too threatening or off-putting about me, although girls' fathers sometimes act like there is. Girls' fathers are like that around most guys, and I don't blame them. In most cases they are interacting with the dude who is screwing their daughter, and they know it. That's just how it is these days. Sex comes pretty easy, or at least that is my experience. I have seen the old movies with guys getting worked up over the girls and the girls playing hard to get and not putting out. It isn't like that anymore. Girls are aggressive now. Maybe girls were objectified back in the old days, but now, I swear it is the guys. I can feel women mentally undressing me just about everywhere I go. I get slipped more phone numbers than I want, and I don't think my experience is unusual.

"She's almost ready," the boy said, coming down the stairs.

He crossed the room and offered his hand, an old-fashioned handshake. "I'm Clay," he said. "Hailey's brother."

"Parish," I told him. "Nice to meet you."

"Parish?"

"Yeah. Parish."

"I've never heard that name before."

"You wouldn't have," I said. "I'm new. Remember?"

Another big smile. A grin actually. His grin was even prettier than his smile. I realized I had just learned the definition of *fetching*. Fetching was standing in front of me.

"Have a seat," Clay said, motioning me toward a chair. "I'll keep you company until Hailey comes down."

"All right," I said, taking a seat.

The only thing I could think of to talk about was how astonishingly beautiful the guy was, and since guys don't do that, I was tongue-tied.

"Where you guys going?" Clay asked, after it became obvious I was socially incompetent.

"I'll let Hailey decide, but I was going to suggest the Raven."

"Cool place," Clay said. "Wish I could get in."

"Don't they do underage shows some nights?"

"No. Nothing Strikes Back does, but not the Raven. Gotta be twenty-one."

"Nothing Strikes Back is my favorite club, actually," I said. "But the Raven's got a good band playing tonight. At least I like them."

"Who's playing?"

"Hoi Polloi."

"I've seen them! They're awesome!"

"Your sister like them?"

"I don't think so. She's more into jazz and softer stuff."

"Jazz? Really? I wouldn't have guessed that. But I just met her recently. Haven't talked much. That's what tonight's all about, getting to know each other."

Clay just smiled, said nothing.

"Maybe I better change plans," I said. "If you don't think she'll like the band."

"She would probably like watching the drummer."

I was surprised he said that. The drummer always performed with his shirt off, the only member of the band who did. And he was drop-dead gorgeous according to every girl I'd ever taken to see them. It was true. He was. But I'd never heard a dude acknowledge his appeal.

"Maybe I should rethink this plan," I said. "Taking a girl to see a hot guy onstage. Hmmmm...."

Clay laughed. "You've nothing to worry about," he said.

I wondered what he meant by that.

"*Hi,* Parish!"

This was Hailey, entering the room with more enthusiasm than the occasion seemed to call for.

"Hey," I said. "You ready?"

"All ready," she said. "Sorry I kept you waiting."

"Clay kept me company," I said.

Hailey rolled her eyes. "In that case, I'm *really* sorry I kept you waiting."

I looked at Clay. No reaction. I suppose he was used to it. I opened the door for Hailey and was about to follow her through when I felt a hand on my shoulder. I turned.

"Don't forget to mention the hot drummer," Clay said.

I stared at him a second then shut the door, joining Hailey on the porch.

"Where we going?" Hailey asked.

"I was thinking of a little coffee house across town," I said. "Sometimes they have live jazz."

"Sounds lovely," Hailey said. "But shall we eat first?"

It was nine fifteen, and I had expected she would have eaten already. Lucky for me I had changed the plan. I would probably have enough money to take her out to eat and to the coffee house if I didn't eat much at either place myself, but I doubted if I had enough in my wallet to pay for our meals plus the live show at The Raven.

I opened the car door for her, and as I did, I looked back at the house to see if we were being watched. I didn't see anyone. For just a second, I thought how nice it would be if instead of this date, I was picking up Clay to go watch Hoi Polloi rock the Raven. The simplicity of that plan appealed to me. I loved that band. Had I known Hailey wouldn't like them, I would have picked another night for our date so I wouldn't miss the band. Maybe I should toss it out there to see if she was interested. I could mention the hot drummer. Awkward, but I could do that.

Nah. This girl wanted to eat.

Chapter Two

Hailey definitely loved jazz and loved ordering the most expensive items on the menu. She also definitely loved having sex. We did it that first night after spending a couple of hours at the coffee house. I invited her over. My place wasn't much—small and in a seedy part of town. But it was all mine--I wasn't sharing--and I kept it clean enough that girls didn't freak out when I brought them home for sex. This happened frequently. As I said, Hailey was the latest in a long string. But the girls weren't dumping me because I was cheating on them. I wasn't. I only hooked up with one girl at a time—it was a policy of mine. They were dumping me because after a while they got tired of me and wanted to be have sex with someone else for a while. At least that's how it seemed. The truth is, I couldn't figure it out. All I know is I always got dumped.

Hailey was better than average in bed. She cost a bit as a girlfriend, but she made up for it. She was worth the expense. I fell for her quickly, the way I did with all my girls. Maybe that was my mistake. Seems like girls want to be treated badly these days, want guys to play hard to get, almost like they are doing the girl a favor by having sex with them. Maybe they are. My problem is that I always fall in love and want to treat them right. So, I treat them right and get dumped.

I had been dating Hailey for about three months when one day I went by to pick her up, but she wasn't there. She was supposed to be; we had a date. Clay, who answered the door, said she'd left about an hour ago.

"Did she say where she was going?"

"No."

I could see there was something he wasn't telling me.

"Break it to me, Clay. Did she leave with a guy?"

Sheepishly, Clay said, "Yeah."

It hit me hard. It always does. Seeing the alarm on my face, Clay said quickly, "Hey, teach me to drive."

"Shouldn't your father do that?" I asked. I knew he had one. I had met him. He didn't live there with the family, but he lived in town.

"He's too busy," Clay said. "My father's a shit."

"Sorry."

"Don't be. Just teach me. I'm sixteen, and I need to learn."

"What year are you?" I asked.

"A junior."

"I figured you were older."

"I'm old enough."

I let that pass. "Okay," I said. "I'll teach you."

I handed him my keys. Clay got the biggest grin on his face when I did that.

"*All right!*" he said with gusto, as if to confirm that he really was sixteen.

He already knew how to drive. That was clear enough from the beginning. But I played along with him and pretended to teach him while he pretended to learn.

"Watch the brakes," I told him. "They've been acting up a bit."

"Thanks for the warning," Clay said.

We drove around aimlessly, our conversation only about driving. It was boring, and yet it wasn't.

"You're doing great," I said.

"Thanks."

"When will you have your own car?"

"Who knows? Hailey doesn't even have one yet. Mom can't afford one and Dad won't buy one. He spends all his money on his other family."

"Oh."

That would suck.

"Hey!" I said. "Stop sign!"

"*I'm trying! The brakes!*"

We were heading down a hill. Our road emptied into a busy four-lane street at the bottom of the hill with a creek running alongside it on the other side. Clay kept pumping the brake and getting nothing. I could see we would be running the stop sign.

"Turn right and pray that nothing's coming."

Clay screeched the car around the corner, hitting the median and bouncing back into the left lane. He flicked on the turn signal, pulled into the right lane, then found a parking lot to pull off the road. We coasted to a stop.

I was embarrassed for my car but mostly just relieved that neither of us was dead.

I looked at Clay, who smiled and said, "I think I'll let you drive."

We laughed.

"Oh, jeez!" I said. "I thought we were goners!"

"More scared than I've been in a while," Clay agreed.

"The brakes had been a little sketchy lately, but I didn't expect them to just totally quit on me."

"Oh, they didn't! They quit on *me!*"

Clay got out so that I could switch seats with him.

"You trust me to get us back to your house?" I asked.

"I trust you."

"With your life?"

Clay said again, "I trust you."

I suddenly realized what I had here. A friend. He may only be sixteen, but he was a friend. A pretty good friend, in fact.

"I trust me too," I told him. "But I think the brakes must be goners. They weren't responding at all, were they?"

"Nope."

"I could tell. I'm not even going to try it."

I didn't have a lot of aces up my sleeve in life, but I did have a few, and I played one of them now. My uncle owned a tow truck. I called him up, and he agreed to give me a free tow. Only thing was I had to wait until he didn't have any customers waiting or until he closed up shop, whichever came last. He said it would be a couple of hours at least. When I relayed this news to Clay, he said he'd better call his mom and let her know where he was. She insisted on picking him up right away. When she arrived, I thought about asking if Hailey had come home, but I knew the answer, and I didn't want to embarrass anyone, especially myself.

Instead, I said, "Hello."

"That's what you've been driving my daughter around in?" she asked, sweeping the length of my car with her glare. I knew her car wasn't much better, but I also knew that the point was the brakes, not the car.

"It's all I've got," I said feebly.

"And now my son?" she added. Then she turned to Clay.

"Why were you with him?"

"He was giving me driving lessons," Clay responded.

"You know how to drive," she said. "Get in the car."

I felt bad for him, his mother exposing his lie like that.

With Clay in the car, his mother had one last question for me. "Why did you offer to give him driving lessons?"

I could have said "I didn't." The truth would have set me free but would have entrapped Clay. How would he explain asking me for lessons?

"I was supposed to pick up Hailey," I said, loud enough for Clay to hear. "She wasn't there, so Clay was helping me kill time until she showed up. He said he could use some practice. I think he was just trying to be nice to me."

"I see," his mother said.

I could see too. I could see that she knew Hailey had unceremoniously dumped me without even bothering to tell me or cancel our date. She immediately changed her tone.

"Would you like to wait at our house? I can bring you back over here later to meet your uncle, or he can pick you up at our house on his way."

"Thank you, but no, I'll just wait here with the car."

"It's probably better."

"Probably."

As she pulled away, I glanced just once at Clay in the passenger seat. He was staring straight ahead, looking mortified.

I knew how he felt. I could remember sixteen. Come to think about it, I had been humiliated myself, coming to pick up a girl who already had left with another guy. Thing was, I didn't feel humiliated, just disappointed. I was getting too used to being treated like this.

No more girls, I told myself. But I knew it was an empty vow. I was addicted.

Chapter Three

While waiting for my uncle, I made some calls and arranged to switch shifts with someone at work the next day. The next morning, I was at the auto parts store as soon as they opened, buying new brakes. I knew they were all shot. I was replacing all four. With barely enough money to pay for the brakes, there was no way I could afford to have them installed. I carried them home, went inside for a water bottle, then jacked up one wheel of the car just enough that I could squeeze under it. I took off my shirt so it wouldn't get grease stains, then I spread a tarp on the ground so my bare skin wouldn't be scraping the gravel. I hated being underneath a jacked-up car. It's dangerous. But after lowering myself to the ground, that's exactly where my head and torso were soon enough.

I hadn't been working long when I heard someone walking up my driveway. I thought maybe it was my uncle, stopping by to see if I could use some help. On second thought, that wasn't likely. He had done me a favor the night before, and it wouldn't be like him to offer another any time soon. I wouldn't ask either, unless I was desperate like last night. I could tell he had always looked down on my family, although just like with the girls dumping me, I had no idea why.

"Need some help?"

The voice surprised me, delighted me actually, but I made certain I didn't show it.

"I might," I said. "How did you get here?"

"How do you think?" Clay asked back.

"That's a long walk. Two miles at least. How did you know where I live?"

Clay pointed to my dashboard. There were envelops on it with my address. He must have memorized it when he was in the car.

"What if I wasn't home?"

"I figured you couldn't get far."

"True, but I could be at work. I could have gotten a ride."

"I didn't think of that."

"So, what are you doing here?"

"It's a Saturday."

"I know that. But why are you *here?*"

"I came to apologize."

"For what?"

"For me. For my mother. For my sister. For my whole friggin family."

"You don't need to apologize for them."

"I feel like I do."

"You don't."

"Then I'll just apologize for myself. I'm sorry I lied to you."

"Forget it. You were just trying to take my mind off being stood up. I got that." I knew that wasn't really it.

"I guess."

There was an awkward silence.

"What can I do to help?" Clay asked.

"Just stick around in case I need you to hand me something."

"All right."

We didn't talk much after that. Clay was intelligent enough to know I needed to concentrate, and I did for a fact. I had never installed brakes before, although I'd watched others do it. With brakes a guy can't afford to make mistakes.

Clay stayed with me until I finished, almost three hours later. He was good company, staying silent when I was working, then offering up decent conversation between wheels when I would rest a moment.

"Hoi Polloi are playing Nothing Strikes Back next week," Clay said after I finished the third brake.

"I know," I said. "I'll be there. I'm not missing them again."

"Can I come with you?"

I hesitated. I had planned to invite a friend of mine I hadn't seen in a while. But I didn't know if he would like the band or not, and it would be nice to see them with someone who was actually a fan.

"Sure. I'll pick you up."

"Thanks!"

He was obviously stoked, and I liked the idea too, the more I thought about it. I liked to let myself go a little crazy sometimes when I listened to live music, and Clay, being sixteen, shouldn't mind that at all. It should be fun. Then I thought of something.

"I'll pick you up on the corner of your street," I said. "I'm not knocking on your door."

"Hailey?"

"Of course. Too awkward."

"I understand. Why did she break up with you, anyway?"

"I don't have a clue."

"You didn't ask her?"

"I haven't talked to her. What's the point? We had a date. She not only stood me up, she stood me up to go out with some other guy. Nothing to talk about."

Clay was silent.

"I know who it is. I saw him pick her up. It's this douchebag she used to go out with."

"I don't need to know. I'm over her."

"That was quick. You must not have really been into her."

"I was. It's just that I get dumped a lot--I don't know why--so I've learned to let go quickly. Otherwise I'll go crazy."

"You get dumped a lot?"

"I get dumped a lot."

"*That*'s crazy."

I realized this was a compliment, and not the first one he'd given me, but I didn't respond.

"You're really greasy now," Clay said.

I looked at my arms and chest. It was true.

I got back to work on the final wheel, lowering myself to the pavement, wiggling my greasy torso under the car. About halfway through, I felt something on my stomach.

It couldn't be, could it? But I knew it was. The hand moved across my stomach then down to the top of my jeans.

"Hey! What the hell are you doing?" I asked, coming out from under the car but staying on my back.

Clay looked embarrassed, as well he should.

"What were you *thinking?* I asked, in a softer voice than before.

"I'm sorry," he muttered. "You have nice abs. I like them."

"Well, like them from a distance, dude," I said, giving him my most disapproving look. I wiggled back under the car so he couldn't see my face. I knew I was turning red.

The silence between us was too much for me. I decided to throw him a bone.

"Someone might have seen you," I said. "Be more careful."

He could take that however he wanted. It was something. And it was all he was getting.

"Sorry," he said again.

I kept working. I was angry with him but also feeling a bit sorry for him, though he didn't deserve it.

"Hand me the other wrench," I told him. The one I was using was working just fine, but he didn't need to know that.

"Here."

"Thanks."

It was harder to concentrate now. The dude liked my abs so much he couldn't keep his hand off them. Go figure. The best-looking kid on the planet, and he's feeling me up. Who would've thunk it?

I worked in silence again, glad that this had been the pattern so the silence wasn't awkward.

"I'll give you a ride home," I said when I had finished. "I need to test these, so you might as well be the guinea pig."

"Thanks a lot."

"Just kidding. I'll take her for a spin first, then I'll take you home."

"No, I'll come with, but I don't want to go home yet."

"I've got things to do. I need to take you home, come back and take a shower, then go to work. I normally work day shift, but I traded with someone today so I could fix the brakes. I'm working tonight. I have to be there at four."

"Take me home on your way to work."

I didn't have a good reason to say no, and it would save me time, so I acquiesced. We went for a test drive. Brakes worked fine. Then back at my place, Clay came inside while I took a shower and dressed.

Clay went through my media collection while I was in the shower. I locked the bathroom door, just in case. It took me a while to remove all the grease. When I came out with a towel around me, Clay had two dozen comments to make about music and films. He liked a lot of the stuff I had lying around and was asking to borrow five or six items he wanted to listen to or view. He also was staring me up and down, reminding me that one of the things he obviously wanted to view was me, naked. I said sure, he could borrow whatever he wanted, then I went to my bedroom to get dressed. Again, I locked the door behind me. While I was dressing, I heard him try to turn the knob.

Back in the living room, I expected to find him moody, but he was exactly as usual, talking about the music again, then about going to the show with me the following week. He had plenty to be happy about, I could see. I also could see that the kid didn't mind testing his luck, and I supposed with looks like his, he could get away with it more often than not if he was in the habit of doing it. "*You can't always get what you want*," Mick Jagger sang in my head, but I imagined Clay often did. I could see that my opinion of him was changing by the minute, and not in a good way, the more I considered that he likely wasn't as innocent as I had assumed.

"I need to get going," I said. "You ready."

"No," he answered honestly, "but I know it's time to go."

On the way to his house, I asked him out of curiosity, "Do you ever see your father?"

"Never."

"I saw him once with Hailey."

Clay was quiet.

"I didn't know she ever saw him."

I realized too late I shouldn't have said anything. It was none of my business. But I had stuck my nose in it now.

"You don't want to see him, or he doesn't try to see you?"

"He doesn't try."

"Crazy bastard."

Clay smiled. I realized I had repaid his earlier compliment without even thinking about it. Good for me.

"I don't think he would like me," Clay said.

I started to ask, "why wouldn't he?" but I knew the answer and didn't want to give Clay the opportunity to say it. I didn't want to hear it. Instead I said, "Forget him then," which probably wasn't the best advice to give a son about his father, but it was all I had.

Clay looked out the window and smiled, a forced smile.

I felt for him, but he quickly turned the tables on me. I guess he thought if I could be inquisitive, so could he.

"Why do all your girlfriends dump you?" he asked.

"Hell if I know."

"Don't you ever ask?"

"I used to. I'd always get some lame excuse like 'I'm just not ready to be tied down' or some shit like that. Things I always thought guys said, not girls."

"You don't mind being tied down?"

"I don't mind."

"Sounds to me like you're a keeper. I don't get it."

"Neither do I. If I knew what to fix, I would fix it."

Clay was silent a moment.

"Maybe you're not good in bed," he said, matter-of-factly.

"I'm good in bed."

"Maybe you just think you are."

I thought about that and said nothing.

"Why don't you take me to bed and let me see what I think. I'll give you an honest opinion."

"Why don't you lay off?"

"Seriously. I'll be the girl. You do what you normally do, and I'll let you know if there's a problem."

"What would you know? First of all, you're not a girl, so it wouldn't work. Second, what do you know about good sex?"

"It would work. I know a little."

I thought about what he'd said.

"Did you just ask me to hump you?" I asked him.

I expected him to squirm, getting asked a direct question like that, but he remained calm.

"Yep."

I couldn't believe it. I kept looking at him as I drove, back and forth, the road and him. He stared straight ahead.

"You done that before?" I asked.

"No."

"But you want to? I mean you want a guy to do that?"

"Doesn't have to be that. But yeah, I'd like to make love with a guy. Or at least have sex with one."

"How long have you known you wanted that?"

"Since I was thirteen."

"You done anything at all with a guy?"

"Just messing around with some friends when I was younger. Nothing heavy."

"Inviting a twenty-three-year old guy to bang you is pretty heavy. Coming on to me while I'm sprawled out underneath my car is pretty heavy. You sure you're not more experienced than you're telling me? You said you knew a little."

Clay didn't answer immediately, then he said, "I was lying. I don't know anything. My only experience is like I said, fooling around a bit with some friends when I was thirteen."

For some reason, I believed him. I'm just dumb that way. I felt bad for thinking bad things about him. Clay had been nothing but decent to me. His hand on my stomach and his invitation to bang him weren't called for, but he hadn't meant to be mean. On the contrary, he had gone out of his way every time I'd seen him to be nicer than nice to me. He was just a horny teenager, a forgivable sin in my book. I had been there, done that, made a fool of myself—with older *girls*. That was the only difference.

I was curious.

"Why do you even like me, anyway? I mean, why me?"

"Because of the way you looked at me when we met. It was the same way I was looking at you. I figured there might be something there even if you were there to take my sister on a date."

"You thought wrong," I told him, and I knew it was a lie. I definitely could have sex with this kid if he wasn't a minor. That wouldn't be a problem. But he didn't need to know that. He'd never give me any peace if he did.

We were at his house.

"I'm sorry," he said. "I didn't mean anything."

"Forget it," I said.

He got out of the car and began the walk up the drive. I rolled my window down.

"See you Friday night."

Clay turned around and smiled.

"I'll pick you up at eight so we can get a spot near the stage," I said. "Be looking for me so I don't have to knock."

I watched him until he was inside his house, then I headed for work.

Chapter Four

Clay was out of sight for the next week, but

he definitely was not out of mind. I thought about him often. The black hair, the large brown eyes, the curve of his cheek, the nape of his neck. There was something extraordinary about the way nature had put him together. Hailey had that same black hair, those same brown eyes, but Clay was more beautiful. I couldn't think of another male I would say that about except perhaps the drummer of Hoi Polloi.

And that is exactly who Clay stared at throughout the concert, standing beside me near the front of the stage. My attention was focused on the lead singer because I loved the way he emoted his songs. I also gave the lead guitarist a good share of my attention because his riffs took me places I wanted to go. The band was just damn good.

The drummer was more than adequate with the sticks, but his sex appeal surpassed his skills. I knew that was what was capturing Clay's attention, just as it had with several girls whom I had taken to see this band during the last two years. The drummer was smart to go shirtless on stage; I could see that. The bare-chested musician appeals to straight guys too.

It was great to be hanging out with Clay and have his attention be on someone else for a change. Thanks to that drummer, being with Clay at Nothing Strikes Back was almost normal. For his part, the drummer had girls fawning over him all over the club, as usual, and if he ever gave Clay so much as a glance, I didn't see it.

On the side of me that Clay wasn't was a girl who, like me, had her eyes on the lead singer for most of the show. Between songs, she talked to me, often at the same time as Clay.

"They're amazing," she would say in my left ear as Clay said, "They're awesome!" in my right.

She was pretty. Very pretty. I had the feeling she didn't think I was half-bad either. She seemed to be with the two girls on the other side of her, both of whom, the few times I looked at them, were checking out the drummer or texting on their phones. I could see why the girl was more interested in talking to me than her friends.

As soon as it was certain the band would not be coming back for a third encore, Clay was off to the restroom, giving me a chance to talk to the girl.

"That your little brother?" she asked.

"No," I said. "A friend."

"He's cute!"

"You want me to hook you up?"

"Too young," she said. "But he's definitely cute."

Her name was Linda, and her friends were in a hurry to leave. Before she left, I got her number.

A girlfriend who really dug Hoi Polloi and for all the right reasons. Could that happen?

It was nice driving home with someone who had enjoyed the show as much as I had, who was stoked and wanted to talk about it. Tonight, that was Clay, not Linda, but I had a feeling the next time I saw the band it would be with her.

As we neared Clay's house, his conversation turned from the music to how much he had enjoyed hanging out with me. Then he was wondering out loud if now that I wasn't with Hailey, if we would be seeing each other.

"We can make that happen," I said, "if you want."

"I want."

He took my cell phone, added his number to my contact list, then added my number to his.

"You've got a lot of contacts," he said. "A lot of girls."

"You'll have even more by the time you're my age," I said. "Or boys. Whatever."

"I think you just told me I'm hot," Clay said.

"I think you already knew that."

"I did. I just wasn't sure if *you* knew it."

"I do."

That admission seemed to please him immensely. I thought it should be enough for him, enough for one night, the concert, me giving him my number, and now the compliment, but he wanted more.

"Can we go to your place?" he asked.

I wasn't sleepy, but I also didn't want to have to drive him home later. I had limited myself to one beer at the club since I was driving, but I had planned to drink a couple more at home while listening to some tunes. Clay would have enjoyed listening to the music with me, but I didn't want to be driving him home after drinking three beers. There were going to be a lot of limits to this friendship. I didn't plan on being a bad influence.

"No," I said. "I have to work tomorrow morning. Need to get some sleep."

It was true, even if I didn't plan to go immediately to bed.

Clay didn't protest.

"Thanks," he said when I dropped him off.

"Enjoyed it!" I said, meaning it.

I watched him walk up the sidewalk to his front door, thinking to myself that I could make love to that boy any time I wanted to, if I ever decided I wanted to. Maybe I should do it now before I started dating Linda. Once I started with her, she would have me all to herself until she dumped me.

No. I knew if I did it with Clay, it wouldn't be a one-off. I would show him the same loyalty and treat him with the same respect as I did my girls, and he might never dump me. I also could get into big trouble if anyone found out. What the hell was I thinking?

I drove off with some intensity, burning rubber. I don't normally do that. I just needed to get away quickly. The only problem was, the person I was trying to get away from was myself, and I was in the friggin car!

Chapter Five

It wasn't long before Linda and I were a steady couple, but much to my astonishment, sex was not included. She wasn't an easy lay, and after dating her for two months, I still hadn't passed third base with her. Part of me appreciated her for that. It was great that she was keeping it interesting, building the suspense. But part of me was going nuts because I was used to having a girl around for sex, even if the relationships never lasted. As long as I was trying to bed Linda, I couldn't bring myself to be screwing around on the side, even though several ex-girlfriends called me up during this period to see if we were still friends.

"I guess," I would say.

"Friends with benefits?" they would ask.

And I would hang up even though I was horny as hell. I wasn't playing the slut game.

In the absence of a woman, I was masturbating at least twice a day, and on a few of those occasions, I let myself fantasize about Clay. I wasn't surprised that making love to him in my fantasy world got me off. Be it Linda or Clay or some of my exes, it didn't matter who I had sex with in my fantasies. The result was the same: I came. As an experiment, just to see where I was sexually these days, one night I tried fantasizing about the Hoi Polloi drummer. Didn't work at all. Clay was the only guy who worked for me, or at least the only guy I had met so far.

Meanwhile, I kept thinking about what Clay had hypothesized. Maybe I wasn't good in bed. I watched some porn. I didn't see anything in the videos that indicated there was something I didn't know—at least nothing that I *wanted* to know. I thought about it. I enjoyed foreplay. I was fit. I took it slow and made sure the girl got hers. I was all over the girl, up and down. I always made sure my breath was fresh, and I thought I was a good kisser. Size wasn't a problem. I wasn't huge, but I was all right. I just didn't see how I could be bad in bed, but damned if I knew why girls kept dumping me. Had to be something.

Finally, it happened. Linda stayed the night with me and we made love. Unfortunately, throughout the sex, I kept thinking of what Clay had said about me possibly being bad in bed. It was inhibiting. I wished he hadn't planted that thought in my head. I thought I had investigated the possibility, analyzed it, and dismissed it, but it was still there haunting me.

Linda, thank goodness, seemed more than pleased with me, as I was with her. This relationship just might go somewhere, I caught myself thinking. Hoping. Now that I didn't have to wait any longer for the sex, I was glad we had waited. We had gotten to know each other. We had a lot in common and had come to accept and even appreciate our differences. That was important.

The months flew by, and Linda hung around. We were having sex regularly now, although neither of us said anything about living together.

I rarely saw Clay, but we stayed in touch. He would call me up sometimes. We also ran into each other at Nothing Strikes Back on occasion, and we could count on running into each other every time Hoi Polloi played that club. When that happened, Linda was percipient enough to find someone she knew to hang out with so Clay and I could have some buddy time. I suppose it helped that during most of the time we were dating, I rarely hung out with my male friends my own age. I didn't have time or maybe I wasn't interested, but whatever the reason, if I wasn't with Linda, I was usually home by myself just chilling.

Aside from those infrequent and unplanned meetings at Nothing Strikes Back, Clay and I never hooked up. The last two times I had seen him at the club, he had a friend with him, his age, who was almost as attractive as Clay. I could see that he was letting me go, and I knew it was for the best for both of us. There was nothing about his friend that suggested he was into guys. He didn't stare at the drummer like Clay. Still, Clay gave his friend as much attention as he gave me, so there was the chance they were dating. I hoped so, for Clay.

When Clay turned seventeen, I decided to do something for his birthday. I called him up and asked him to meet me at a nice café near his house. I bought him a meal and gave him some tunes I thought he would like. He was looking better than ever, if that's possible, and now that he was a bit older, he didn't seem quite so off limits. But I had Linda, I was happy, and I think I've established that I'm not a cheater. Besides, maybe he had rescinded that offer by now.

"You seeing anyone?" I asked. I couldn't help myself.

"No," he said, and I saw a glimmer of hope in his eyes. I shouldn't have asked that. "You still with Linda?"

"Yeah. Imagine that."

We both laughed.

"What about the guy you were with at the club?" I asked.

"A good friend, but just a friend."

"Does he know you're gay?"

"What makes you think I'm gay?"

We laughed again.

"So… does he know?"

"Yeah, he knows. He's cool with it."

"Good to hear."

Fortunately, there was no drama that evening, just a nice, casual meal together and a bear hug—our first—as his show of appreciation that I had remembered him on his birthday.

I wasn't surprised that he remembered mine, as well. Clay called me up and asked me to meet him at the same place. We had another nice, casual conversation, and he gave me some tunes that I already had. I didn't tell him that. He mentioned that he would be getting a car soon, finally, and asked if he could stop by some time.

"Sure," I said. "Any time."

As it happened, Clay stopped by on a night I was expecting Linda. She had been a bit distant for most of the week; I wasn't sure why. To make sure things weren't heading south, I had bought her a dozen roses and cooked dinner, so when the doorbell rang, expecting her, I opened it wide and thrust forward the roses. Needless to say, Clay was quite surprised.

"Oh. Hi," I said. "I was expecting Linda."

"I can see that," Clay said. "Smells good."

"The roses?"

"Yes, they do, but I meant the smell coming from your kitchen."

"Oh. Yeah. Just seafood pasta. Nothing too fancy. Cooking isn't one of my strengths."

"Smells delicious. I'm sure she'll love it."

I didn't want to invite him in. I didn't want him to be there when Linda arrived. Consequently, I left him standing there at the door in limbo long enough that he got the message loud and clear.

"Well, I'll be going," he said. "I can come back some time when you're not busy if that's all right."

Halfway through his last sentence, my phone rang. Instead of answering him, I looked at the phone. Linda.

"Hello?"

Clay waved goodbye and started to walk away, but I motioned for him to stay so I could give him an apology and a proper goodbye. Obviously, Linda wouldn't be showing up at any minute if she was calling, and I felt bad about not inviting him in. Thus, Clay stood waiting as I talked to Linda. Or rather, as she talked to me.

I suppose my face said it all. Or maybe it was me dropping the roses on the floor. But I suppose really it must have been my watery eyes and the fact that I couldn't speak.

The phone went dead, and I just stood there, not knowing what to do.

"She didn't," Clay said.

I nodded that yes, in fact she just had. I knew I should be more than used to it by now, but for some reason this one really hurt.

"Do you want me to stay or do you want me to go?" Clay asked.

I thought about it.

"Stay."

Clay shut the door behind him, stooped to pick up the roses.

"You hungry?" I asked.

"I could eat."

We went to the kitchen, where the table was set and waiting. I had bought a fairly expensive bottle of wine--expensive for my budget, in any case. As Clay filled his plate, I uncorked the wine and poured a little into his glass then quite a lot in mine.

"Aren't you eating?" he asked.

"Not hungry," I said.

Clay ate.

"This is excellent," he said. "You don't give yourself enough credit. And thanks for letting me have a little wine. It's good."

"That's all you're getting since you're driving. Besides, according to the laws of this country, I would be contributing to the delinquency of a minor and all that. You know."

"Not much of a contribution," Clay said, holding up his glass and smiling. "But thanks."

"You're welcome."

"The laws of this country are messed up," he added.

I knew he was talking about more than the wine.

We were silent for a while.

"You didn't see this one coming, did you?" Clay asked.

"I never do."

"Was it an anniversary or something?"

"No. I just felt like doing something special for her."

"You're such a romantic. I love you."

I stared at him. I couldn't help it.

"I would never do that to you," he continued, looking me in the eye. "If we were together, you'd either have to break up with me or put up with me forever."

I knew this was true, had always been true. My head was spinning from Linda dumping me, from the wine, which I had been drinking quickly, and now from Clay, leveling me with his truth. It was too many conflicting emotions. I couldn't speak.

"You sure I can't have some more wine?" he asked when he saw that he had melted my heart.

"No. You've got to drive home."

"I don't *have* to drive home. I could spend the night here."

"What will your mom think if you don't come home?"

"I'll call her and tell her the truth, that I'm staying with a friend. I do that now. I'm almost eighteen, you know."

I didn't answer. I went to the bathroom to pee and wash my face. When I came out, Clay was standing in the entrance to the kitchen waiting for me. I stopped where I was, so it was Clay who walked across the room until he was standing directly in front of me.

I stood there, watching Clay unbutton my shirt. I let him take it off me. We were staring into each other's eyes, then Clay dropped his gaze to look at my chest and abs. He put his hand on my stomach. I remembered the time it had been there before. I paused, wiped my eyes, then lifted Clay's shirt over his head. He had seen my body before, most of it, but I had never seen his. He was lovely, just as I expected.

Again, we stared at each other, and I knew there was no going back. When one foot is in paradise, the other soon follows.

"So, this is my lucky night?" Clay asked, still staring.

"No," I said. "It's mine."

Updates to some of the characters in this story can be found in the novel *Jeremy Bardon* by Luke Hartwell.

About the Author

Keith Hale grew up in central Arkansas and Waco, Texas. He received his bachelor's degree from the University of Texas at Austin. Following a five-year career as a journalist in Austin, Amsterdam, and Little Rock, Hale earned a Ph.D. in literature from Purdue and took a position teaching British and Philippine literature at the University of Guam. Hale writes both fiction and scholarly works including his groundbreaking novel *Clicking Beat on the Brink of Nada (Cody)*, first published in the Netherlands, and *Friends and Apostles*, his edition of Rupert Brooke's letters published by Yale University Press, London.

Houseboy Wanted

The author is looking for a houseboy, age 18-30, to help around the house and with driving. This is a legitimate position. In exchange for cleaning; some cooking; some work in the yard; providing a daily shoulder, neck, and back massage (so the author can continue to write); night driving, and providing good company, the person hired can expect free room and board in the two-bedroom, full bath upstairs, a small stipend, a friend, a writing mentor (if desired), and possible help with local university or trade school tuition once in-state residency is acquired (if desired). You should be dutiful, considerate, easy to live with, interesting to talk to, a nonsmoker, and pleasing in appearance. Race and sexual orientation are nonfactors. If interested, send a self-description, at least one photo, and your stipend expectations to: johnnykhale@gmail.com

Titles by Keith Hale

Fiction

Clicking Beat on the Brink of Nada (Cody)
Heart and Soul
Truck
Nothing Strikes Back
Space
Breathless
Yusuf Parish Jimmy

Nonfiction

Books

The Bisexual Brooke (from Rupert Brooke of Rugby)
Edleston: Lord Byron's Boy Poems
Friends & Apostles: The Correspondence of Rupert Brooke & James Strachey, 1905-1914
Hafiz & The Lover Divine
In the Land of Alexander: Gay Travels in Hungary, Yugoslavia, Turkey, & Greece
Ode to Boy: An Anthology of Gay Literature
On Love & Youth: Three Translations of Sa'di
Rupert Brooke of Rugby
A Survey of Gay Literature: From Homer Through the 1st World War
Torn Allegiances: The Story of a Gay Cadet

Introductions, Forewords, & Afterwords

Arms & the Boy: The Poetry of Wilfred Owen
For the Love of Moses: A Shropshire Lad & Last Poems
*Georgian Poetry: A Compilation of Georgian Poetry,
1911-1922*
The Hill: A Romance of Friendship (Horace Annsley
Vachell)
Our Mutual Friend (Dickens, Watersgreen House
edition)
The Portable Rumi (Watersgreen House)
The Professor's House (Cather, Watersgreen House
edition)
Sonnets to a Young Man (Shakespeare)

watersgreen.wixsite.com/watersgreenhouse

Watersgreen House is an independent international book publisher with editorial staff in the UK and USA. One of our aims at Watersgreen House is to showcase same-sex affection in works by important gay and bisexual authors in ways which were not possible at the time the books were originally published. We also publish nonfiction, including textbooks, as well as contemporary fiction that is literary, unusual, and provocative.